ARTISTS & ALCHEMISTS Publications

Art is transformation of material & the Self

215 Bridgeway, Sausalito, CA 94965

Words by *Donna Ippolito*

Erotica

Drawings by *Adele Aldridge*

Calligrapher — Moira Collins

ISBN: 0-915600-00-5

Library of Congress Catalog Number: 75-10048

All material copyright © by Donna Ippolito & Adele Aldridge, 1975.
All rights reserved. No part of this book may be reproduced in any form without the written permission from Artists & Alchemists Publications.

for our friend,

ANAÏS NIN

who said,

"... Man fabricated a detachment which became fatal. Woman must not fabricate. She must descend into the real womb and expose its secrets and its labyrinths. She must describe it as the city of Fez, with Arabian Nights gentleness, tranquility and mystery. She must describe the voracious moods, the desires, the worlds contained in each cell of it. For the womb has dreams. It is not as simple as the good earth. I believe at times that man created art out of fear of exploring woman. I believe woman stuttered about herself out of fear of what she had to say. She covered herself with taboos and veils. Man invented a woman to suit his needs. He disposed of her by identifying her with nature and then paraded his contemptuous domination of nature. But woman is not nature only.

She is mermaid with her fish-tail dipped in the unconscious. Her creation will be to make articulate this obscure world which dominates man, which he denies being dominated by, but which asserts its domination in destructive proofs of its presence, madness."

and,

"I will never be able to describe the state of dazzlement, the trances, the ecstacies produced in me by love-making. More than communion, more than any joy in writing, more than the infinite, lies in the unity achieved by passion. It is the only moment when I am at rest, that is the summit, the grace, the miracle."

THE DIARY of Anais Nin, volume two

Erotica

I watch the moon sprout to fullness
    and dream my hair woven with thistle.
Night after night I watch,
    eyes hard & bright with desire.
An ache
       a sob
           sap bursts in my ears
  in my knees
          in my quivering thighs
and I swallow the moon
which passes through its phases
in a sudden blinding flash.
Ripe & stuffed with light
    my body glows on all & none.
I want men now not by their names
    but by smell or voice
    or the grace of fingers.

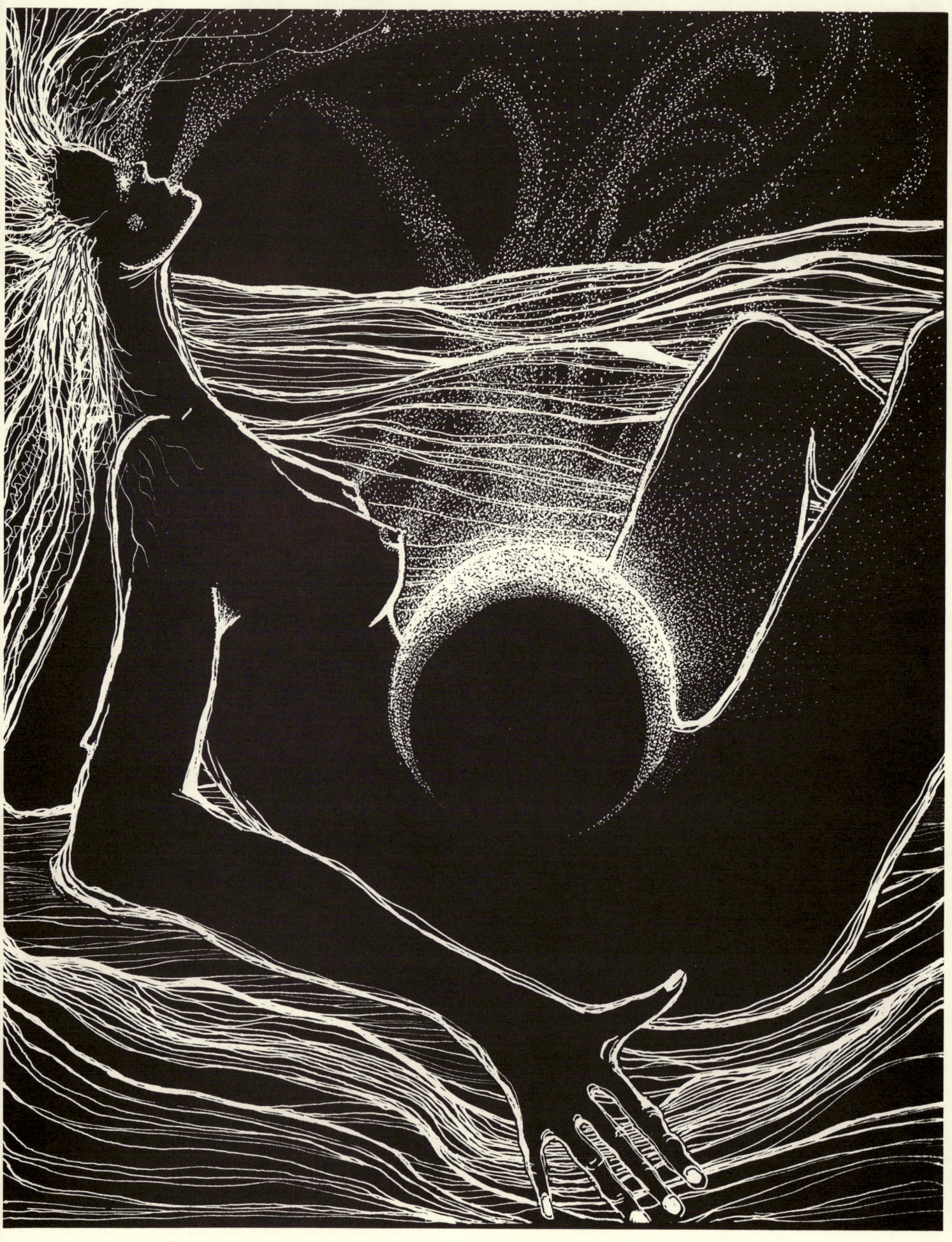

And I love them
>   all their necks and gesturing hands
>   their mouths smiling
>   phrasing
>   their sleeves rolled up to the elbow
>   their clothes making me want
>   them naked
>   want to undo their shirts
>   and put my lips against shoulders
>   or the tight flesh of their backs
>   making me want to open my legs
>   and take them in
>   with a little gasp of pleasure.

They speak & emphasize with an open palm.
I stalk the gesture of unconscious fingers
>   and dream my breast within
>   their curve
>   feel the hand
>   both hands
>   gently holding my buttocks
>   or touching my inner thighs.
Dark & rimmed with silver
>   I look then at their mouths
>   and the backs of their hands,
>   at their hips,
>   the sling of hips,
>   long step,
>   strong thighs for me to kiss
>   and with each I listen closely
>   only to their laughter.
>   x x x

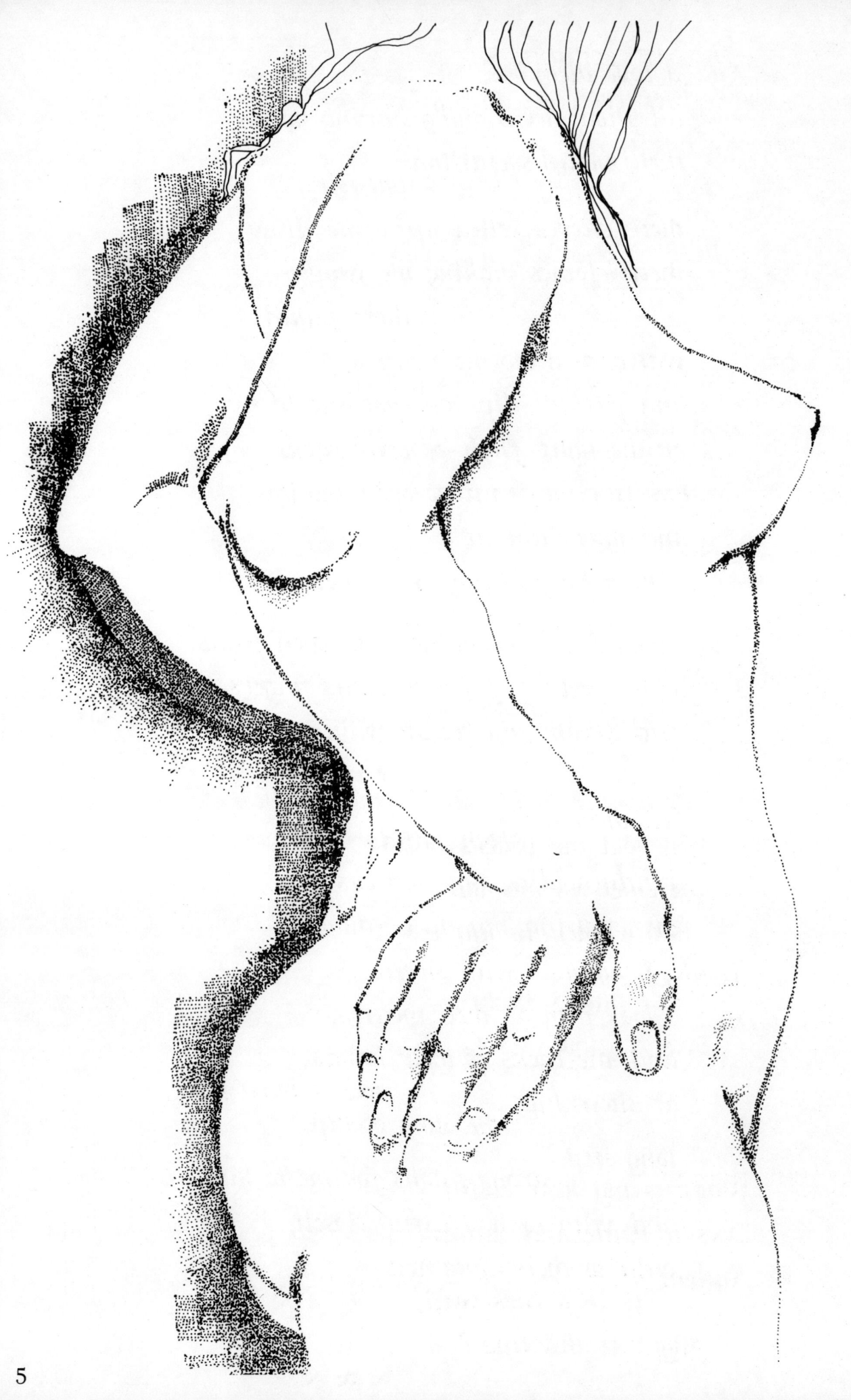

The cat screams,
    her call like an infant screech.
So blunt
    so starved,
        it frightens.

And I
    do I strut along fences
    then crouch in corners
    flicking my tail in longing & fear?
And mine,
    what is my screech?
Do I howl by night over backstairs
    beckoning to any tom?
Am I a bitch,
    the blood smell all over the block?
What is my heat song?
Is my desire a harsh edge of voice
    a twitch of hips
      something in the way I plant my legs
      or hold my breasts?
Is the smell in my hair,
    is the smell in my pits?
Is it soft,
    talc & herbs?
No
  Does it glow
      does it singe
          does it burn?

What is my heat chant?
Does it rattle and taunt?
Ancient,
    is it a cat's wail,
    night frightening?

                x x x

Undressing alone, I undo
    unbutton more slowly,
    feel the brightness of flesh,
    sudden breasts lifting,
    then back sweet-curving as I bend.
Naked all alone and I love the muscle,
    strong hinge between hip and thigh,
    then all down my legs from walking.
Naked all alone
    skin nerves
    quick against me muscle spring
In my body. In mine.
In my skin, sheath surface sensor,
    feeling there the loving touching.
There there I am touched
    and it is the skin giving.

I am ripe.
My body is sharp & ripe as oranges,
    juicy, the belly more curved, thighs soft.

I am a shape in nature
    and my hips widen like seeds,
    a pear tapering,
    a bank of earth rising.
I am a shape in nature
                    a cunt
    and have round hips & thighs & buttocks.
I am a shape in nature
    drifting like snow
    spreading in leaf
    curving like light & space.

I touch myself.
Hair, handfuls thick & heavy like rainy earth.
Face, where I am behind. Brows, sweet fuzz,
cheek fragile
nose sturdy
bone.
Fingertips, my own tracing my face,
make me soft.
Dare I do I love my body?
Fine dark hairs from my navel
to the wild shrub of cunt
rise & fall with the belly breathing.
Brown moons bright around my nipples
grow too and recede with breath.
Dare I love let love for my body warm me
relax the cunt
flow from my cunt,
warming
relaxing the rest of me,
tingling even my toes.
Dare I do I love
let love breathe from my cunt?

Listen.

So fierce
the body sizzles.
Changing
mixing
spitting
solving, dissolving, resolving
taking me making me.

Nerves crawling blood beating
    through miles of body
    making red making red
    beating at the fragile wrist.
At my pulse
    I strain to hear its tiny thud.
A flutter
    insect feet
        my pulse that I touch,
    listening as it begins to pound at my ears
    hurting
        monotone
    too strong
    too strong to bear
    too much
        my own pulse
    the force of my own life
    my body.
It grows,
    a soft mad static,
    sensation of my pulse
    and my body seems to grow hot.
The monotone beat the beat the
    endlessness of the pulse
    it beats me.
My own pulse
    the body's song
    is blood and beat
    endless beat of blood.

It bears me
        becomes me
    and I am always becoming
    my body my blood becoming
    breath beat beat
    breath beat beat breath beat beat breath
    beat beat and breath.

I know
        I sing
            I embrace my body.
Sinuous
        blue yellow red
            striding.
Daring me
        daring.
A sunflower
        big-headed, brassy & tall.
To the light
        always to the light.

                x x x

We sit before the fire,
   our bodies dark eerie & copper by its light.
I lean back & you hold me,
   hands spread over my belly,
   just touching the underside of my breasts.
You take my hair in your hands
   untangling
         drawing it down
   touching a place on my spine to mark its fall.
Then you begin to brush,
         taming my hair.
Smoothing
      your free hand follows the brush
   and it is as though you caress
   the moss between my legs.
Stroking
   you draw hair away from my temples
   and my head pours into my hair,
   into your hand smoothing.

My head bent back lets my hair drop long,
 and beginning at the crown you caress it,
 one hand rhythmically following the other.
My fur
  my feathers
     the skin on my back
grow moist with pleasure
     and I turn to you.
Letting your touch slip toward my cunt
 you open my thighs & the fire warms my legs
 which further part.

Gently you roll me onto my stomach,
  lean to kiss my back
     my buttocks
 the inside of my knee.
You pause to lift my foot
  & place your mouth
  and moving tongue against the arch.
I shimmer as your fingertips spiral
  over the length of my body,

as you knead gently
the back of my neck
my shoulders
    spine,
as you trace
the stripe of my butt with your tongue,
from behind finding
the proud red beak of my cunt.
I draw you down beside me
   & touch your cheek
  ear
     chin
        your hair,
admiring the soft angle of shoulder,
your chest so beautifully formed
that the breasts are mounded
    as a woman's.

I touch one
          laughing
                    teasing the nipple
then see suddenly
                not your body
but my own firelit against you.
Startled
      I am caught there
and begin to watch only its line
      delicate
only the floating edge
        of shadow shoulder
                        waist & hip.
This flow of skin
          curve of bone
              stuns in its grace.
Softly breathing & a fragile thing,
    strong wings,
    the silhouette is somehow mine.
I am at once my body & this reflected
    from your warm brown skin.
The shadow lives,
    is me & something more or less or pure,
    bearing me
        giving form.
I am revealed.
I am stillbound,
        never having seen.
White beach
      warm sea
           my seabird
    my effortless body
           the hips slowly move.

              x x x

We lie listening to the music
    and I walk into it,
                    my naked back
    legs & buttocks offered to you.
Tuning
     I let the music lap at my feet,
    remain still as it washes higher
    rising in me
    making me want to take the sound
    into my hips
         arms
              and hands
    while I dance for the sake of the music
    for my sake
           and still dance for you.
Head lowered
        fists loose
I am muscle, knotted calves
    and the weightlessness of balance.
I am a thread of sea grass,
    my body guileless
    revealing its love of self
    my glee in self.
Fringe
    rhythmic
           I sway,
    the heat from my cunt
    nearly buzzing.
And I dance while you watch with anger
    tension
        yearning growing.

And I dance till you spring from the bed
    to stand behind
    penis slipped between my buttocks,
    nestled down to touch the tip ends
    of my pleasure.

Your chest brushes
    your hands are light
        around my breasts
    and I pass my hips against you
    with a gentle thrust.

Legs weak
        I move slowly
                you move slowly.

My nipples flame & the hard seed
            of my clitoris
    seems to lift upward
                hot & throbbing.

I reach back to touch your penis
                which is warm
    a warm petal now
                firm but yielding.

We remain so
    our hands moving over one another
    and my breasts become hands
    that caress your hands.

Your hands become breasts
    that are bell-shaped
    and whose tips are like lashes opening.

Your hand moves down
    the center of my body
    tracing the moist curve with a finger
    that pauses just above my clitoris
    and there is dilation
                  my cunt tastes air.

The window is open & any sound
    could be heard from without.
Remembering the strange distinct
        woman's laughter
    I listened to one night,
    I cease repressing the single
        endless chord.
I moan for the eddy
    the thrill in my nerves
    which gape like beaks.
My pleasure is yours
    and I moan for the sake of moaning.
I babble
      murmur my senses
    & that voice excites
    while the voice of your fingers & your
    warmth and your thighs against
    the back of mine is silent & wild.

Always you are silent
    but for the tiny shouts at my
        first touch

of tongue or hand or fingers
at first entry into my body
at the split second before you break,
coming.
I sing now for us both.
My soft cries beg you to answer
direct your movements
direct mine.
More than anything I sing
to make you reply.
I want my voice to take yours & make it
speak call cry sing your body.
Oh yes, yes
& there & there & there.
Be there be there & please answer me
sing with me
lift with me
rise with me
wing with me.
Play with the wind.
Single-minded
it slams at us.
We let our taut bodies strike against it.
We flatten
we dip
we drift
we try to touch down
and new currents lick us higher.

I caw
I croak
and always you are silent.
I am a pistol shot repeating.
x x x

I kiss the shadow on your hip,
    touch & follow it into the gritty curl,
    fingers tangling in the hair,
    then take the heat of your penis.
Very deliberately I close my hand,
    softly
        less softly
            firmly
    moving slowly down.
My tongue follows
    first tasting with rapid flicks
    the smooth oval tip
    and with the same flicks
    following the shape down & up,
    then swifly
        lightly
            all around.
My tongue speaks without words
            of tenderness.
My tongue sings without words the body.

The flicks gradually begin
        to dart & pierce
    as they touch & I am glad
    to nibble gently at your balls & hair,
    glad to take the warmth of your penis
    into my mouth.
Eyes closed,
    you lie still,
        shuddering
    but holding still.

My arched breasts, the hungry nipples,
　　strain against your chest.
Your worn & powerful hand cups
　　　　　　one taut breast
　　the cool tongue flashes at the other.
The cool tongue laps at one nipple
　　the warm fingers feather the other.
Is it fire? is it pain? is it a leaf
　　or rain or sand or is it breath?
Is it more is it more is it is it more
　　and more and more?

A small knot lifts my clitoris.
I feel it swell
　　　　simmering
　　　　　　　vibrating
　　　　　　　　　hot.

My hips move like fins.
Supple
　　strong and fluid
　　my hips move of themselves to
　　the throb of my clitoris,
　　to its echo lower
　　　　　　parting my thighs
　　opening my lips.
I hear cries
　　　tiny sobs in my throat
　　　　　　　　on my lips.
I gasp in surprise,
　　　　laugh softly.
I laugh again louder for the pleasure
　　which lifts my hips

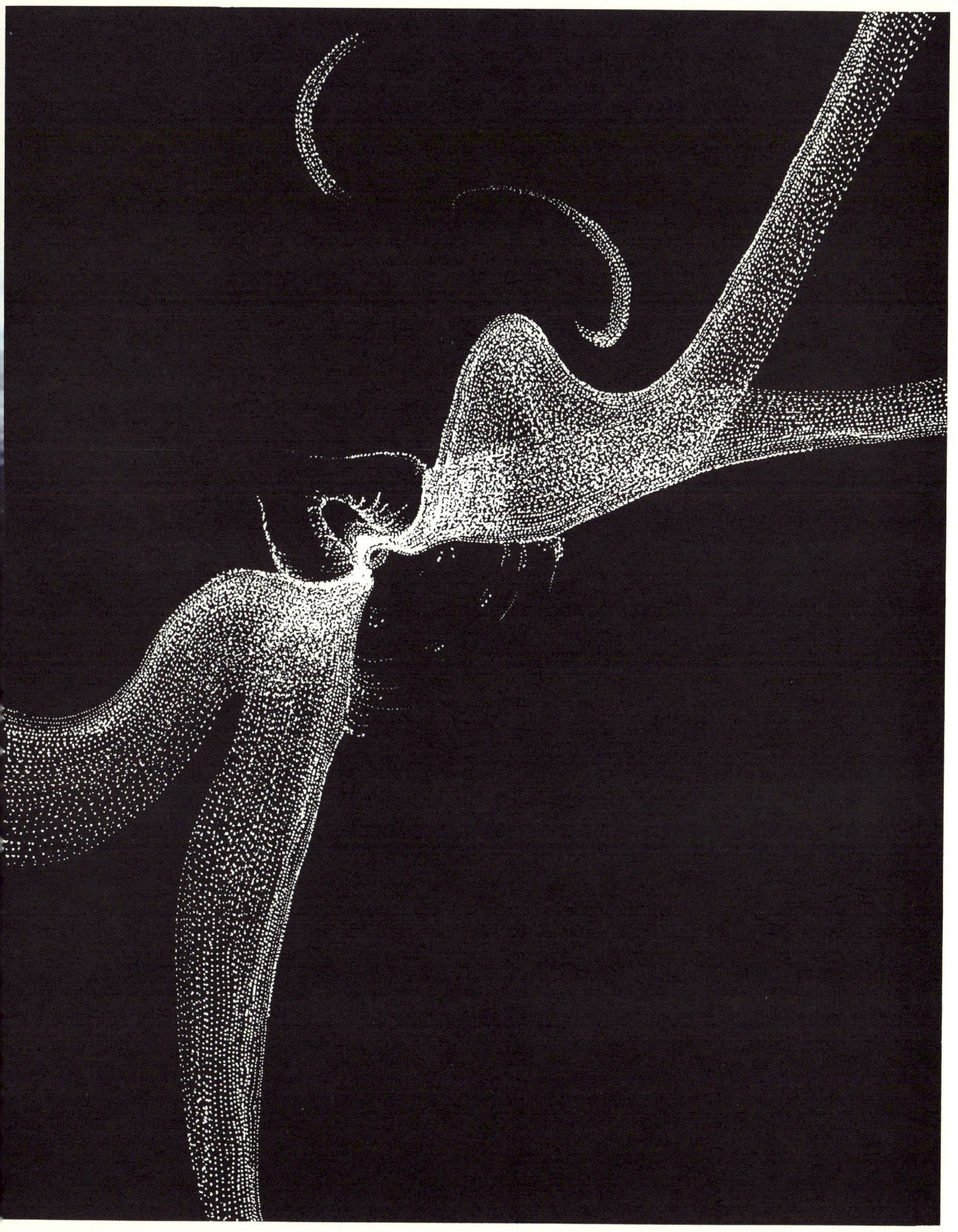

tosses my head from side to side,
and I whisper no oh no no no
I am not deep enough to go so deep
so dark
    so near where she lies
so near where she lies
      the snake
where she lies gleaming
    lying poised to strike.
Leave her
  oh leave her
     leave her lie.
She is death
  is dark swirling to draw you in
  and in and in to the eye of a shell
  beyond the eye and ever darker
  in through till I can hear the
  dark roaring like the sea in a shell.

I turn to you & lay my hand
  on your belly
   just above the dark hair & the small
   involuntary leaps of your penis.
You lie back & my hand seems to grow hot,
  my hand seems to flame from your body
  as I let it slide lower.
I take your penis firmly but lightly,
  taking it to meet my mouth & tongue.
You shudder
    head thrown back
    against the pillow.

I smile as your pleasure washes over me
        and I watch my hand
        caressing you erect.
I moan
      hold you & press down slowly
    with two hands tenderly cupping
   down
      down
          down.
I watch your face.
I pant
    demanding that your closed eyes
    your ecstatic mouth
    shatter & dissolve before me.
Now now now.
Now still the eyes
        the mouth
    your limp fingers lie rooted to pleasure.
My thigh is flung over yours
    and I begin to move softly
    brushing the whole of my pubic crest
    over your warm smooth skin.
I go slowly
      still watching you.

                x x x

Don't give me poetry.
I want you vulgar
    want you to curse me
    as you strain to be closer
    deeper in me
    getting lost in the caves of desire
    my insatiable desire.
I want to devour you.
I want you to hate me at the moment
              you come,
    as the thrusts of your body name me
    as the only possible woman
    the only living woman.

Sliding down to the bed
    I draw you over me
    take you fragile but erect inside me
    and whirling my hips I end
    with a stab against you.
Spreading my legs,
   feeling myself open like a greedy mouth,
I whirl again
   stab stop & whirl & stab.
Over me you are helpless & heavy
   while I turn my hips like a rushing wheel
   which can do nothing but wildly spin.
I pull back my legs & brace for an instant
   before I lift & nearly throw your body
   with my thrusting.

Again again again & I know you weaker
 and weaker against me.
You moan
 moan again
 gasp.
I go faster, know my strength
and gleefully bounce you higher,
 harder & harder.
You utter little sounds of surprised ecstacy.
All the while my cunt grows deeper
 still deeper & you begin to move too.

I am exultant
 then begin to rock
 let your stabs rock me while
 I make room inside for you.
Again I meet your thrusts with my own,
 going first joyfully counter time,
 then joining your rhythm
 letting my hips dance against yours.
I am open,
 am air burst from a bubble,
 and know there is more,
 still more space for you within me.

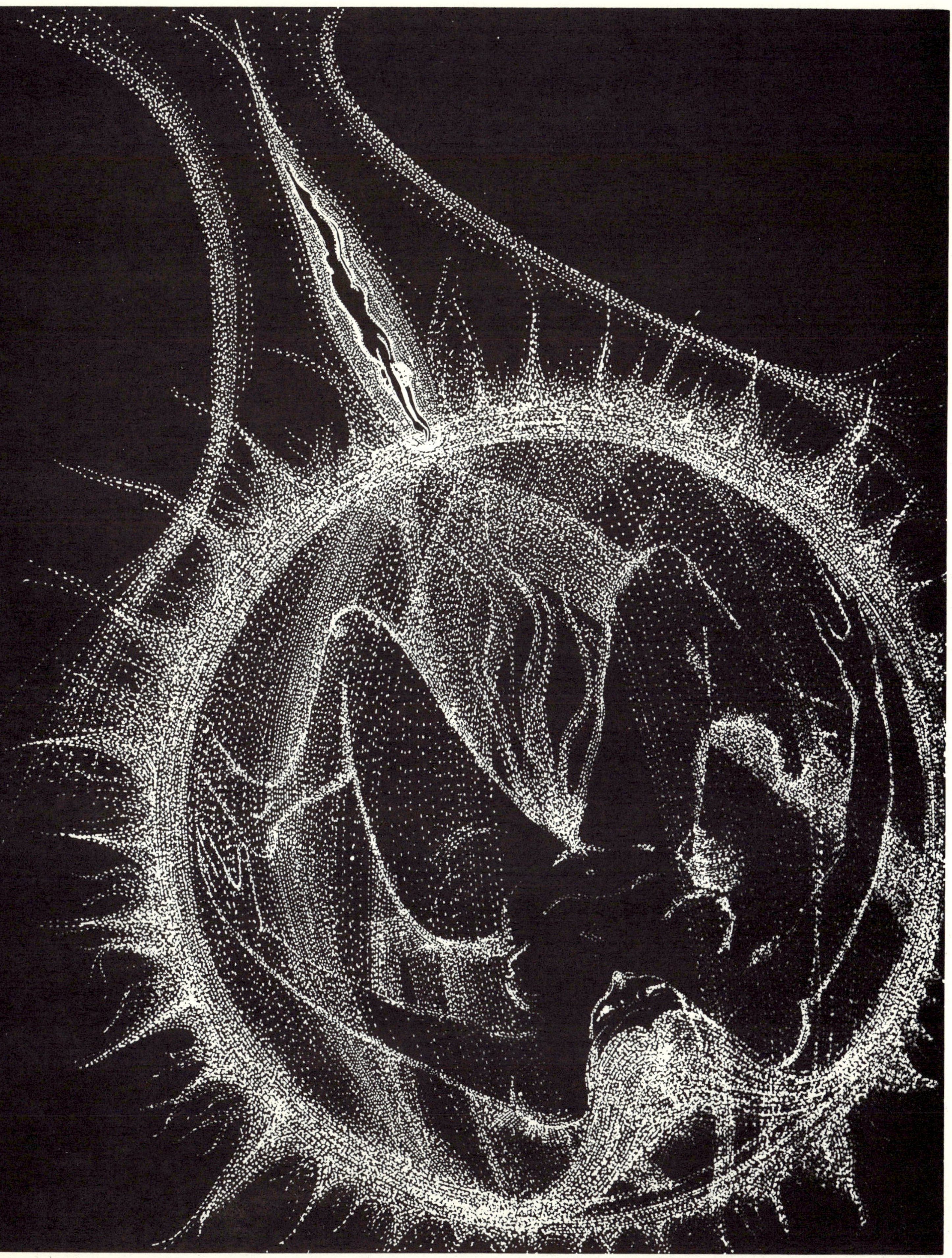

You stop,
       hold your thighs, knees
     legs & feet
               tightly clasped together
      holding me
           lying still
      pressed hard into me
      & very still.
I wait
     out of breath
          and smile into your hair.
You do not speak
    and I revel in the hardness of your body,
    the tension by which you stand between
    your strength & my body,
    its webs all torn.

You cry out in delirium & I begin to move.
My hips whirl, spin, wind.
My hips thrash at yours now lashing back.
You raise yourself slightly
               look at me

36

then throw back your head at the
same moment you begin to thrust into
me at the same moment my hips rise,
my legs spreading further apart,
to meet the thrusts
                    the ramming almost
that grows faster
                more abandoned.
You sweat
        you frenzy
                you shriek in whispers
you burst against me
        shaking my head
                      and arms
        and hands crazily
        as you plunge.
Yes my body shouts yes I can contain you
    I am deep enough & more.
I pull at your sun-dried hair
        saying fuck me
        yes now yes yes now.

                              x x x

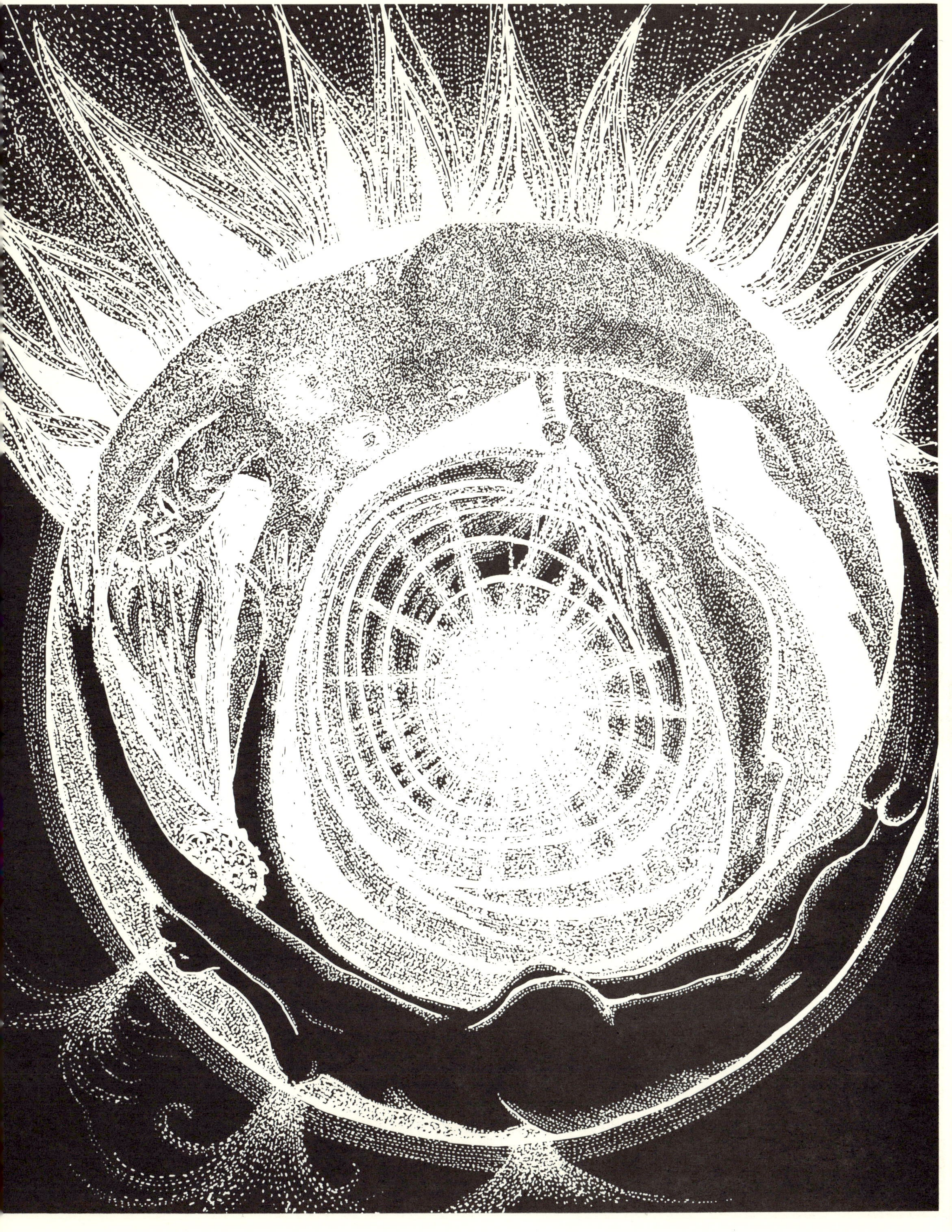

Sensation breaks over & holds me.
I am lace or the rhythm of rain on a pond.
   and know the shifting pattern
   will only draw me deeper in.
Instead I want to leap up with the broad
   muscled legs of a hunter.
I let go the ecstacy of fins
   trail my fingers like a fin
   down your chest
   coming to your thigh
   to your penis
   which I brush
   with moving fingers.

Our lips open & close more
   insistently against the other's.
You stroke one of my breasts
   which are lifted & held high.
You drop every now & then to my hungry
   cunt which sucks as though your
   finger were a nipple.
The tension which moves my hips
   rings with an echoing
   rapidly sounding clang from the muscles
   in my belly, butt & my thighs flung
      with abandon
   as widely as possible apart.
I stop the movement for a moment
   and you lift your fingers to my breast.

We conspire against orgasm
    as the pleasure at my breasts soothes
    the runaway head
                 the wild mane.
My body whinneys,
    my cunt is the frantic scatter of birds
    before a storm.
My own movements,
    the touch of air even at the inner lips
    of flesh make me shudder with pleasure,
    and my body is tinder again.
You press both hands to my inner thighs
    then let them rise to my throbbing cunt.
With a finger of each hand you stroke,
    then slide one finger inside,
    touch the other to my clitoris,
    the tropical name of a flower.
The musk of our sweat
                your semen
    my secretions
               mingle & intoxicate.
I am blood
           I am at the first moment
                        of breath.
I ignite with a blinding explosion.

                x x x

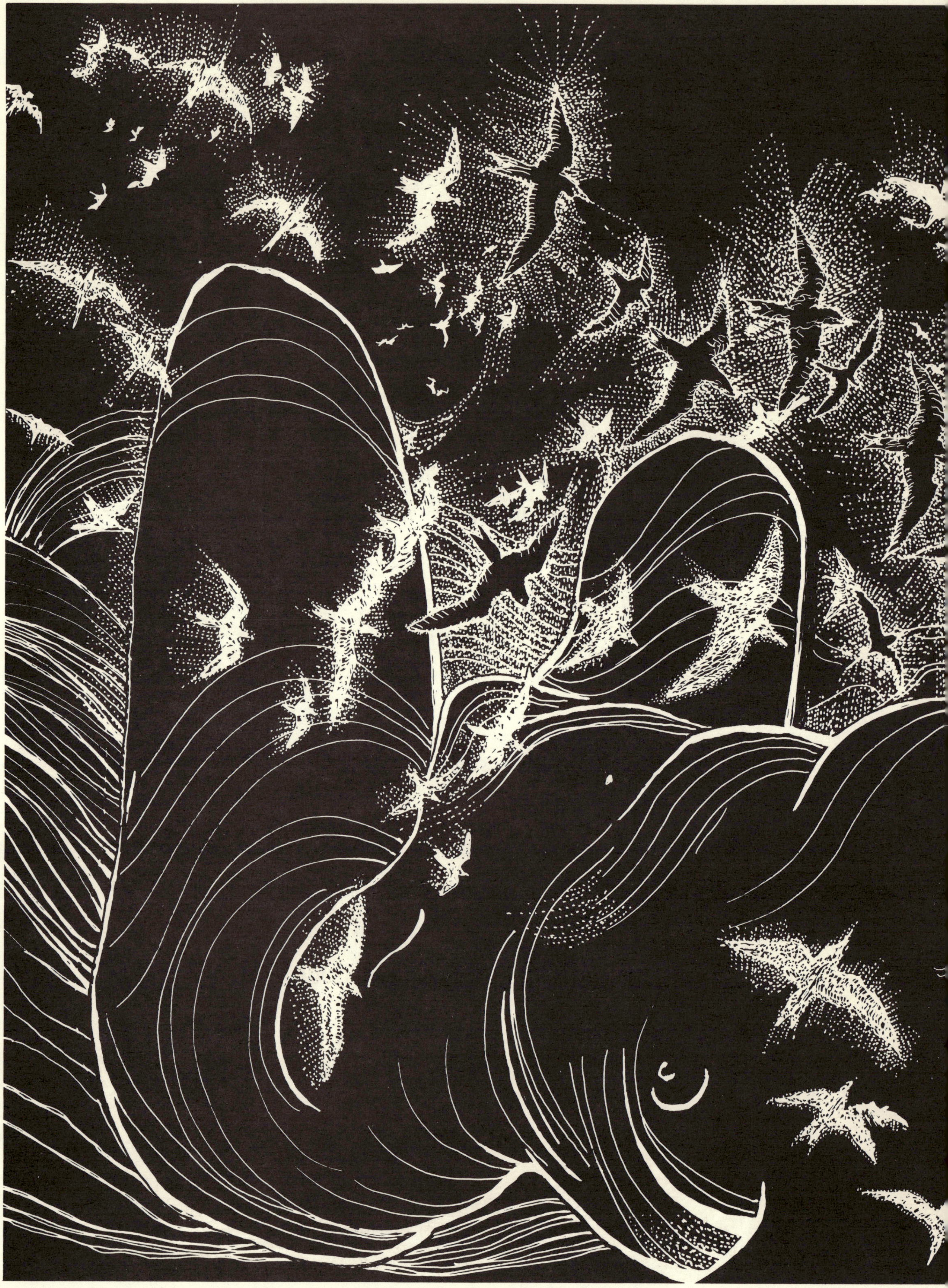

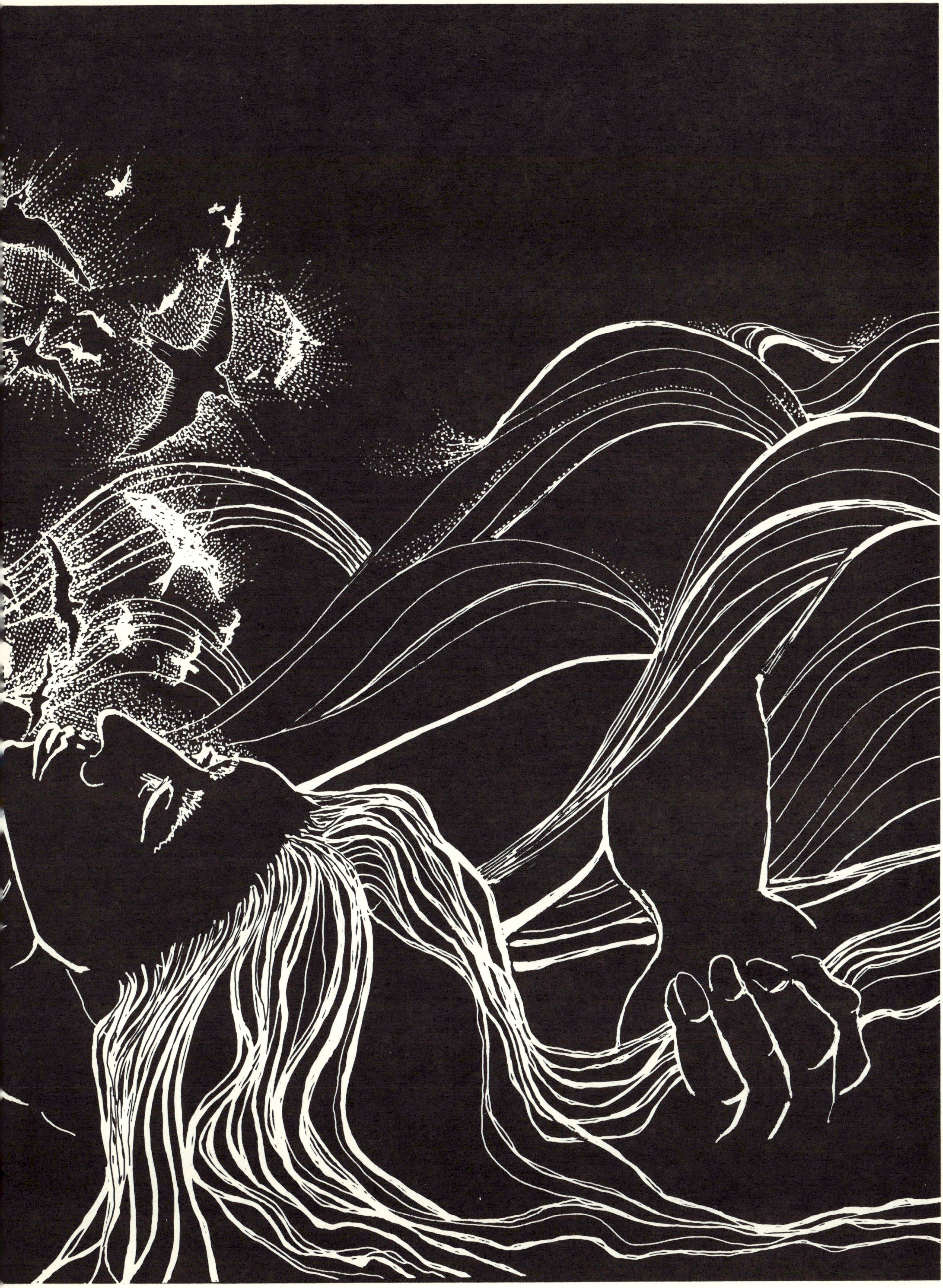

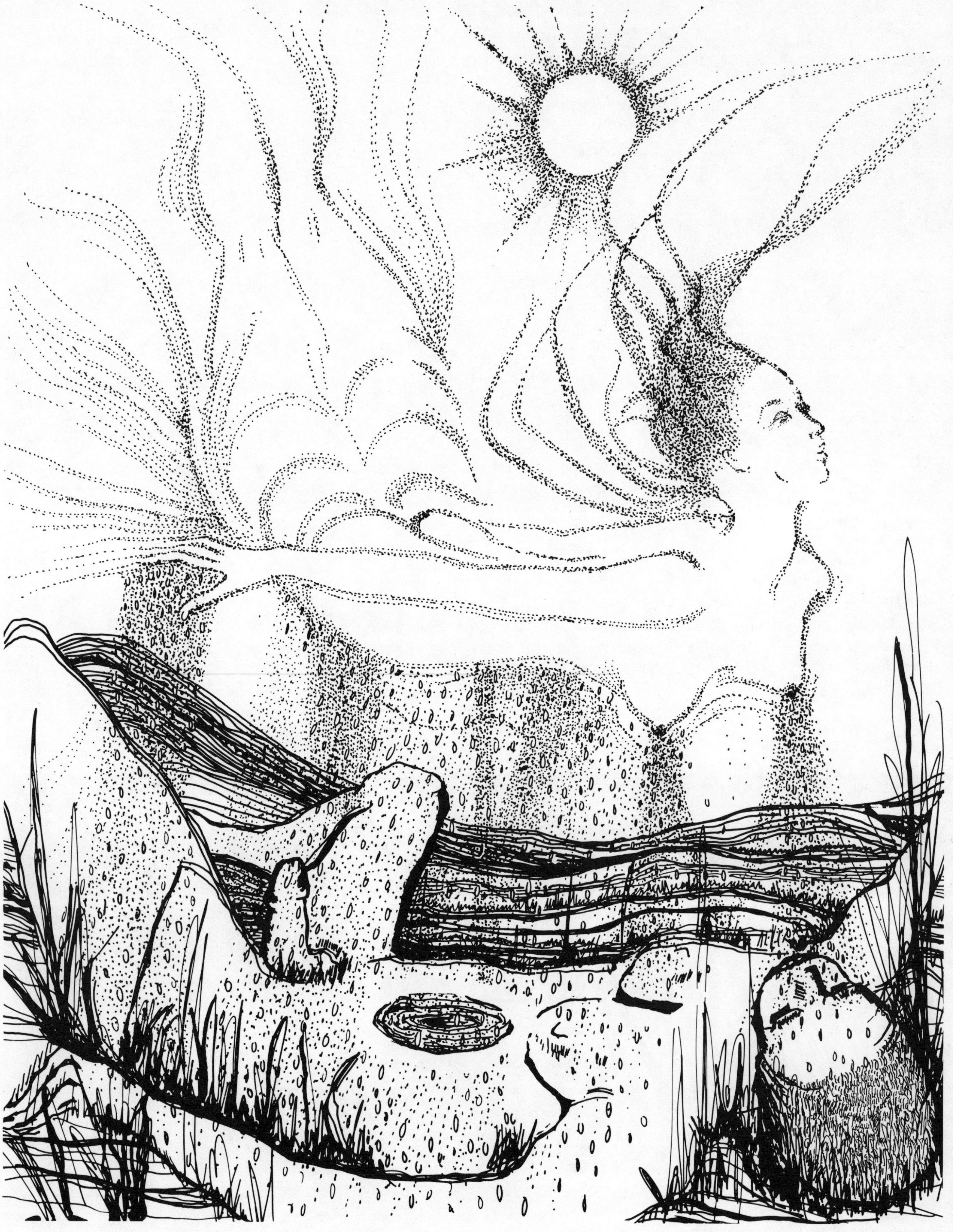

Your hand lifts to caress me
                but I turn it away.
What rises to my throat is the body,
      its passion for movement & power.
What moans at my throat is the body,
      carven & smooth as jade.
My breast against your mouth, your hair,
      and you fear me.
Catching your thigh between my legs,
      my hips saddle you,
                guiding
                        cantering
      rocking your movements to mine.
I hold your penis still
      moving my cunt over it
      letting the juices come.
I press the tip to my clitoris,
      and our wetness keeps us gentle
      though again & again I press.
I love your cunt, you say,
      and, like fingers, the words excite.
I am astride
      pouring my cunt over you
      shaping myself to you in undulation.
You are still
              I in motion.
I am still,
          daring you to ride into me,
      my cunt supple & deep,
      eluding & containing your thrust.

Our hands sweat
                skins stick
     and my fingers squeeze softly,
     open slightly your buttocks
             as you probe
     as I challenge
     as our bodies run together then
speeding
         slashing.

But I am more quick
     and can slow you suddenly
     to another stride where I lick you
     with my inner lips
     soothe you with the muscled hand
     of my cunt to say there is more.
Deft as insects
            our bodies shift
     and I straddle you yet
     my back now to your fore.
Opening even further my thighs
     I am buoyant as we rise & fall
         like breath
     while I can feel your pulse ever
         harder inside me.
My power exposed freely in every muscle
     every line
             every movement of my body
I am vulnerable,

Stronger & stronger
     your blood beats
     at my cunt.
With small gestures
     I rein you again.
You draw me down so I lie above
  my back to your chest
  my hips still holding your penis
  my cunt arched & accepting
     your thrusts.
Abandoned to my body
  to your pleasure in my body
  I break free from its pod
  my seed fibers streaming
     like milkweed.

Catch me
  catch me
    catch me if you can
  sings my nether mouth
  and your thrusting grows
  more frenzied, more involuntary.
But I love the chase & shift again.
Under you now,
  my cunt bounces like sun on water,
  blinding as your penis
  reaches out to seize.
I want you fleet
    or not at all.
I want you swift as a shorebird
  rhythmic as a gull.

Before we are done
> I will know you dancing to my body,
> caught under but joyously bearing.

Before we are done I will know you soaring
> your body sleek in its spasm.

Before we are done I will know you light
> heady as woodsmoke.

Before we are done
> before before before we are
> done, we are done, done
> before we are done I will know
> you fearsome
> I will know you furious in grace.

x x x

48

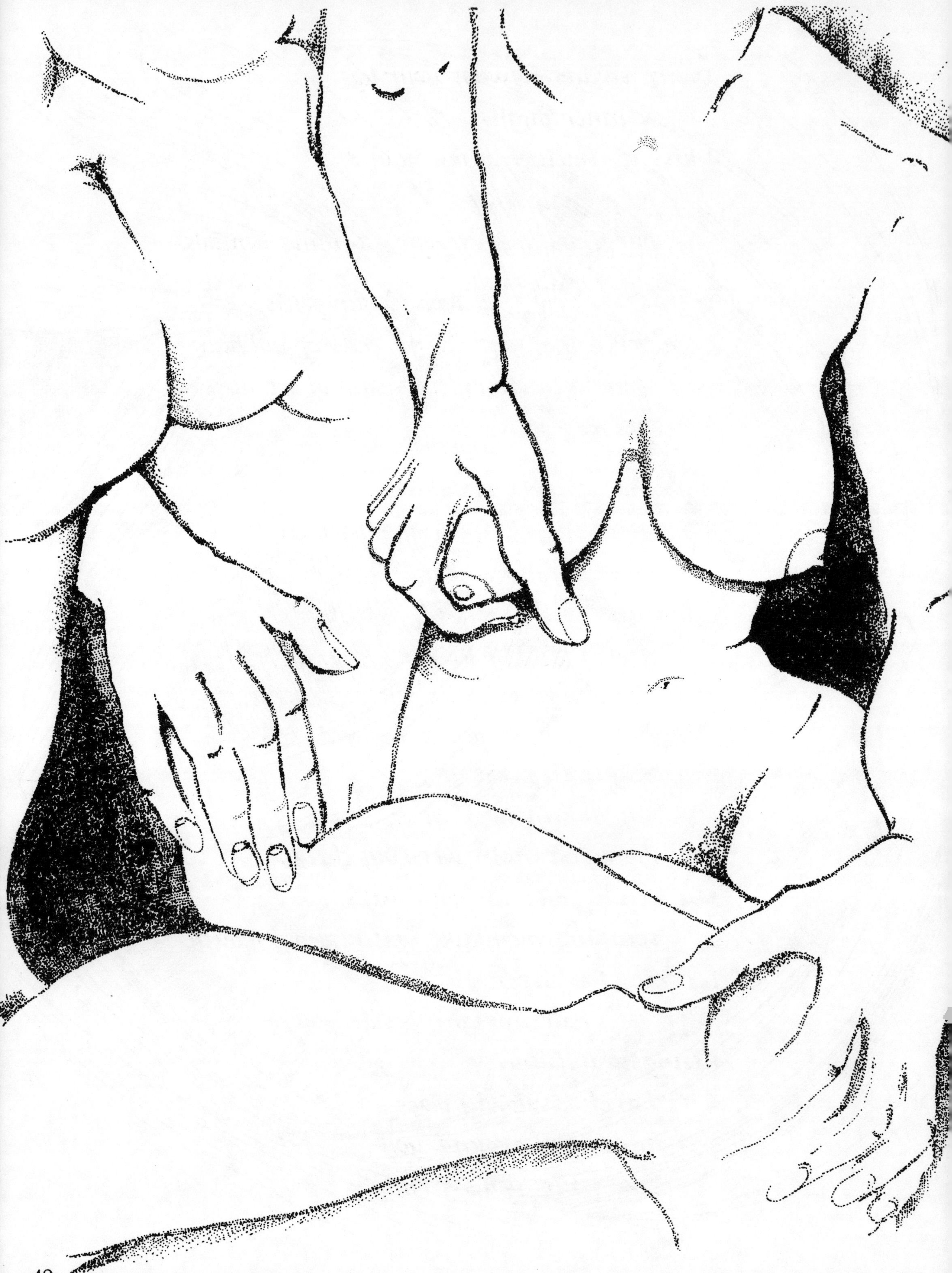

Desire sweats between your legs
    & inner thighs.
I kiss it, smell, rub my head &
    hair against it,
    bury my face in your steaming genitals.
Leaning forward,
    I wrap your penis
    for a moment in the ends of my hair
    and kneel beside you, saying let me
    just be still
        and let me.
The line of your shoulders
    your chest tapering to slender hips
    your thighs so hard & firm
    move me
    and I bend to kiss.
Hair winds from your chest to belly,
        gentle mound.
My tongue licks at it
    my mouth wets it
    the moist hair wets my cheek.
My hands take up your balls
    scooping them like water to my mouth.
Let me, I whisper,
    half upright beside you.
Rising to my knees
    I arch & slowly place
    my thighs around you,
    take your penis firmly.

Trailing it through the swollen lips
    of my cunt
        I place its tip inside.
With a shudder I seize you
    my thighs tight to your hips.
As I draw you in
    there is a sensation of coolness
    and I feel friendly for a moment
    and affectionate.

I hold you still
    hold you motionless inside me
    and you place one hand on each
        of my breasts.
Tantalizing the nipples with the arch
    of your palm
    touching then with your fingertips
    you roll the nipples gently.

Testing my body
    I lift from my thighs growing hard.
Lifting higher
    rising to my knees
    drawing you straight up with me up
    till you have almost slipped out,
    I hold you with the tension from
        my jade room,
    full of whirring birds.

Lowering again
              closing over you
    I soak your penis.

You tap
        press
             tap quietly at my nipples.
You yield to me
              form under me
    and I carry you like a ripple.

And now I love to play
        knowing that the spasm is only a
              breath away
        knowing I have no power nor do you.
There is only this game
        a thrusting into air as children
              do in swings
        testing their grip
        testing the desire to rejoin space
        testing the love of earth
        which pulls us just as
        dangerously close to an edge.
Our bodies poise exquisitely between the two
        moving into flight
        moving into fall
        grasping the swing by its ropes.
We get dizzy
            fall
               seize the air
        with our pumping legs
        as the swing turns up again up.

52

I know the winding will begin.
I know the orgasm is upon me.
It whips its tail like a rattler
    sending a sob of anticipation and
    pleasure through my being.
The heavy throb comes once
    goes
      is gone
          is gone
              oh no gone
    then throbs again
        and goes.
I begin to move
    seeking its rhythm
    its hovering beat.
It eludes
    then tangible
        throb
    a throb of surprise and
    recognition from my cunt.
Throb, throb
    long & slow I undulate.
Effortlessly in & out
    the movement a snake within me,
    I lift and drop around you.
No strain
    nothing but this gesture
    drawing you in
        drawing away
    repeating countless times
    my eyes closed
    my hips & legs circling your body.

            x x x

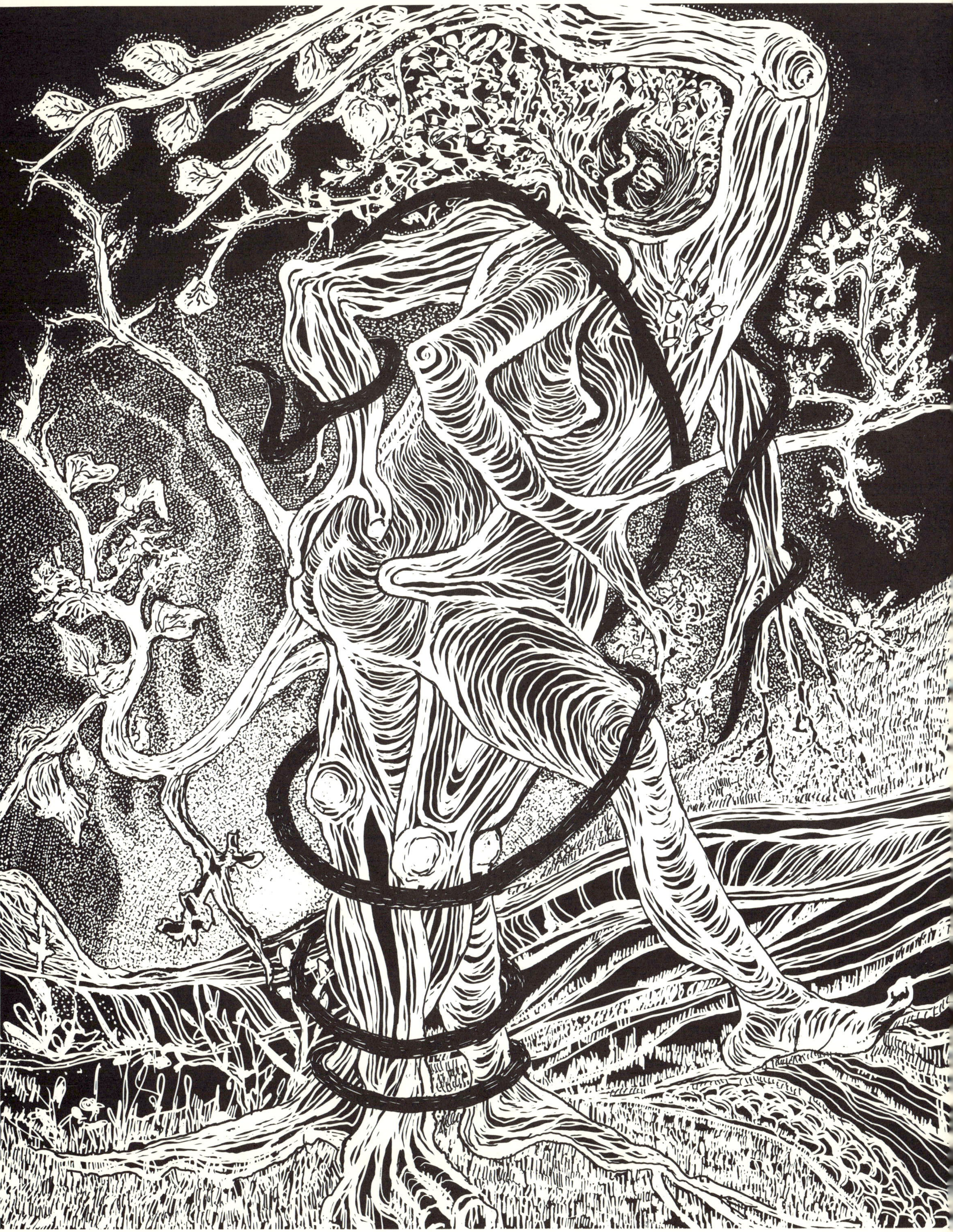

We spread our blanket on the grass
      & wild mint, kneel down & kiss.
Our barely touching thighs,
    bellies & breasts strain
    against our clothes as we continue,
    tongues dabbing like rain to water.
Your fingertips then are light
    at the silk around my breasts,
    the hard nipples,
        and I am silk,
    slipping to the ground,
    my body lying half over yours.
Your penis stirs beneath my hand
    beneath your clothes
    and I breathe deep the smell of mint
    bury my face in your neck & the
        smell of grass.
I laugh to think that someone might see us
    and you are glad.
I am glad someone may see us,
    blessing your touch
    moving like wind over my body.
Your tongue wets the silk of my blouse
    my nipples.
Between my thighs
    your hand lies still,
    maddening.

Near your hand my cunt is the lightning
      tongue of a snake
      while you undo my clothes
      and lay your mouth against
         my throat
      the crown of my breast,
      and I raise my arms to offer
      the underbreast as well.
Your mouth trails softly across my
      bare stomach.
I open your shirt
      and lie again half over you,
      my breast to your mouth which
      kisses, wets & burns the nipples.
Smother me, you say, and I
      crush my breasts to your face
      while your mouth cools
      with its wetness.
My body is ravenous & I lie back
      letting your head move down
      move down to the streak of fire
      from my cunt.
I lie back
      & open my thighs to your mouth
      to the dance of tongue
      and the tip which pries gently
      opens me suddenly

      letting the wind
      the sound of rustling trees
      enter with your tongue.
My cries are the whisper of leaves.
My body soaks up damp earth.

Your lips,
         your tongue against my clitoris
      your tongue inside my cunt.
Or is it a nibbling?
Is it a childish pleasure
      this sigh that relaxes my whole body
      then sets it moving,
      my voice to mournful little sounds
      like a hawk calling far off.
I am the skin of a drum.
I am stringed to vibration.
I am soundless
         quiet & deep.

So rapidly
         your tongue & mouth flash
      at different parts of my cunt.
My strained body exhales again.
Your mouth and tongue are cool
      smooth as flint
      rhythmically touching my clitoris
      and seeming to press when inside
      against a ceiling like a cloud.

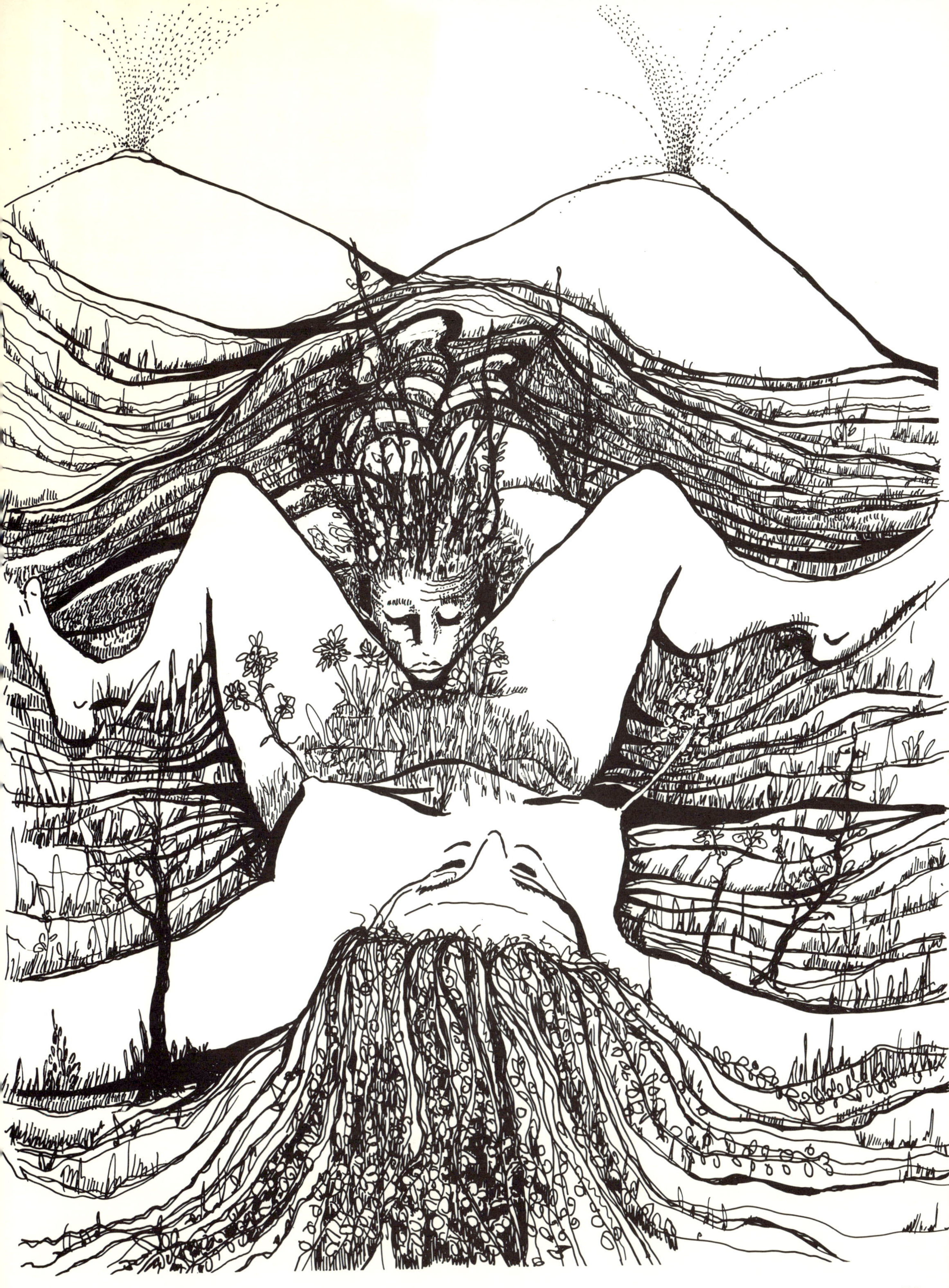

You caress my inner thighs with
    your hair and spread fingers.
I look up into the trees
    throw out my arms to touch the grass.
My sap runs
        the pulse of my cunt races
    and I want it all.
I want your strong thigh against my
    open cunt
    your hair & fingers brushing
    my nipples & breasts
    your tongue beating softly inside me
    your fingertips at my clitoris
    your penis smooth
    as my thighs close over it
    your mouth moist all over my breast
    your back damp & strong
    under my hands
    your hair in my hands
    while your head moves
    to the rhythm of your tongue
    inside me.
My senses gorging
        gulping I want it all
    want your tight finger
    the strain at my thighs
    the soak & smell from my cunt
    the clench of my body
        my clitoris

the pressure like pain
your light spirit tongue
your harsh arrow tongue
my hips lifting to give you the place
the place begging for your tongue
which never stops & my cunt spinning
growing like clay on a wheel
vibrating upward & down
the vibrations tremoring into my blood
my belly
    my legs & feet
        my fingers
my breasts
    my back
        my shaking head & shoulders
my cunt spinning so fast that I shatter
and come shouting.

                x x x

Breathing hard
    my cries dying away
  I yearn for your breath, your mouth
  moaning against my neck.
My sounds soft
  I taste & caress you
  warm & firm as a ripening in sun.
My fingers are madness,
  my cunt against your thigh.

As you relax
           a small smile parts your lips.
My breath quick
           I smile
    and your eyes open to watch
    my mouth
    my tongue
           my eyes watching yours.
More naked than our bodies
    is the look passing between,
    strong thighs opening wider,
    your penis gesturing for my mouth.

My whole body become
    a languorous tongue,
    I know you hardly dare
    breathe or stir.
You submerge
           eyes closed into pleasure,
    and slowing even further,
    we drop deeper into your senses.
Stalking
        deliberate as a cat
    my mouth seeks out
    your hidden spaces
    the pores of pleasure.

your senses suck at me
              slowing
    slowing my breath.

I slip down
      lightly grazing your body
      with my breasts
      & my mouth wants more
    my mouth wants your back

    the fine thistle of hairs at its base
    where I kiss
    moistening the path up your spine.
My mouth wants your scent & returns
      down the curve of your back
      follows the cool mound of your butt
      to the shadow just at the thigh,
      its heat warming me.
Always more,
      my mouth wants
      the high hard muscle of thigh,
      the smoothness where,
      softly biting
      softly kissing,
      I explore to your taut belly.
Still more
      and with small kisses
      I wet your penis down into the hair
      and up again
            down & back again
      to the tip which my mouth wets
      with breath
      which my mouth covers gently
      slowly now slowly sucking.

                    x x x

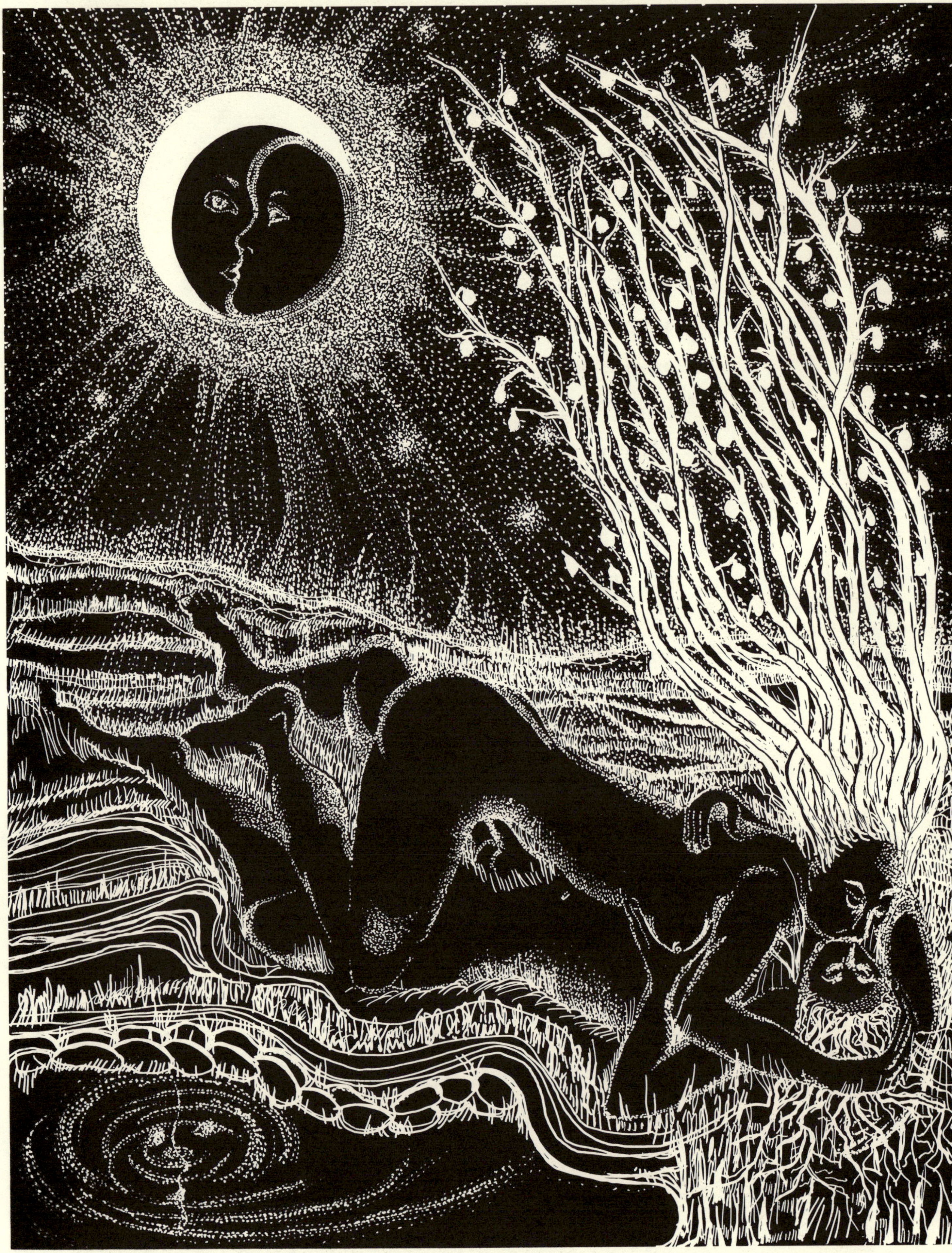

Your body over mine
  and my welcoming thighs
  spread wider.
Anthers drenched
  I breathe open to your thrust
  close as you draw away.
I touch your penis to my clitoris,
  then move it barely skimming
  through my inner lips.
Exquisitely slow
  you enter again
      cry out
  stunning by your hardness
       meeting mine
  and from a dark pinpoint
  the eye of a shell opens
       circling over
  enclosing & offering access to the eye,
  to my cunt flaring open
  quickening & sucking at you,
  the air around you.

Breath hard
   your body is smooth
    poised & taut.
I surge at you
   cresting with my cunt
    slowly against you
  then away.

Coiling
>	my hips are sure & rhythmic
>	the cunt swallowing you
>	then drawing back.
And you begin while I stroke deeper
>	and harder while you answer
>	thrusting long
>	thrusting tense.
Your hips
>	your penis now demanding
>		rapidly jabbing
>	and I only grow more strong & fierce
>	calling you still further
>	with the wildness of my hips.
Wet skin
>	strong legs
>	our embers hotter than fire.
You gasp,
>	arch as though you'd been hit.
Terror
>	hunger
>		the awful scorching into me
>	the rocketing through me
>	to where I am a place
>	no longer a body.
Thrust thrust I exult in every thrust.
Strong thrust & fierce
>	my cunt roars as you bear down
>	face hot against my cheek
>	breath ragged & low
>	your body searing into mine

       scalding against mine
       your body sobbing
       jagged against mine
       hammering at mine.
Again
    again
        again
           again
              and again
   then you are still.
Panting.
So suddenly heavy.
I look up into the trees loving.
I kiss your tangled hair & laugh,
    the low sound strange to me.
One hand still to my belly,
    fingertips just touching
    the low mound of damp hair,
    you lie beside me.
I lift your hand & kiss it
    cupped around my mouth.
To cool my body
    I roll into the grass & mint.

                x x x

Fearful
    wanting to hide my blood
                I lie tight.
Your tongue to me
       licking at my cunt
   everywhere tasting.

Fearful
    I lie tight
              whispering stop
  wont you stop.
I lie tight
    wanting to close my legs
              hide the shame
    the feeling I am an odor & a stain.
I lie tight
    fight the blood
      squeeze shut my pleasure
        hating the blood.
I try to push your head away
    and it lifts to look at me.
    all smudged
          it lifts.
My blood
    is all over your face, I say,
    touching it.

This blood
    this blood
          it must be me.
Woman bound
    breasts swollen
          hips more round.
This blood
    I fight this blood
    squeeze shut my pleasure
    drowned in waterfalls
      spattering red
            blood rapids
    carrying me away,
    their force more than the fear
    and I begin to meet the blood,

unlock my fingers
unlock the terror in my spine my cunt
and stand on the blood
as though it were earth.

Blood soaks the sheets & I don't care.
It's only blood.
It's only my brightness.
It's only the thin wires which feed & heal.
It's only ourselves making ourselves
    thumping through the body.
The pump of blood of hips of air of blood.
Eat blood know blood see blood taste blood.
It must be woman be dirt be stink be cunt
    be woman be ripe be woman be blood.
I am thud of blood at wrist & breast & belly,
    the twitch of blood.
I lie in it
    lie against it on you
    feel it damp
    feel it crusting
    and I know it's only blood.

you wear my stain & I could
    bloody your hair, pale hair,
    with my cunt,
        the blood
            covering everything
    like some kind of joy dust,

    and I open my legs
    offering you not my cunt but
    my blood.
You are so smooth this way
    slippery & deep.
I am barely filled this way
    feeling you more as a coolness,
    a slant of wind.
Glossy
    the blood lifts us
    and you pierce me
    light through a pane
    the pane clear
    the shaft
    the air
    the lucence.

I am alone
    spotting small brilliant flowers.
I am alone
    spilling my cunt.
I am ripe
    trickle warm
    dripping
    and my blood sings,
    the song slapping between us.
Naked
    stark
    I am blood fresh
    my body moving like blood.

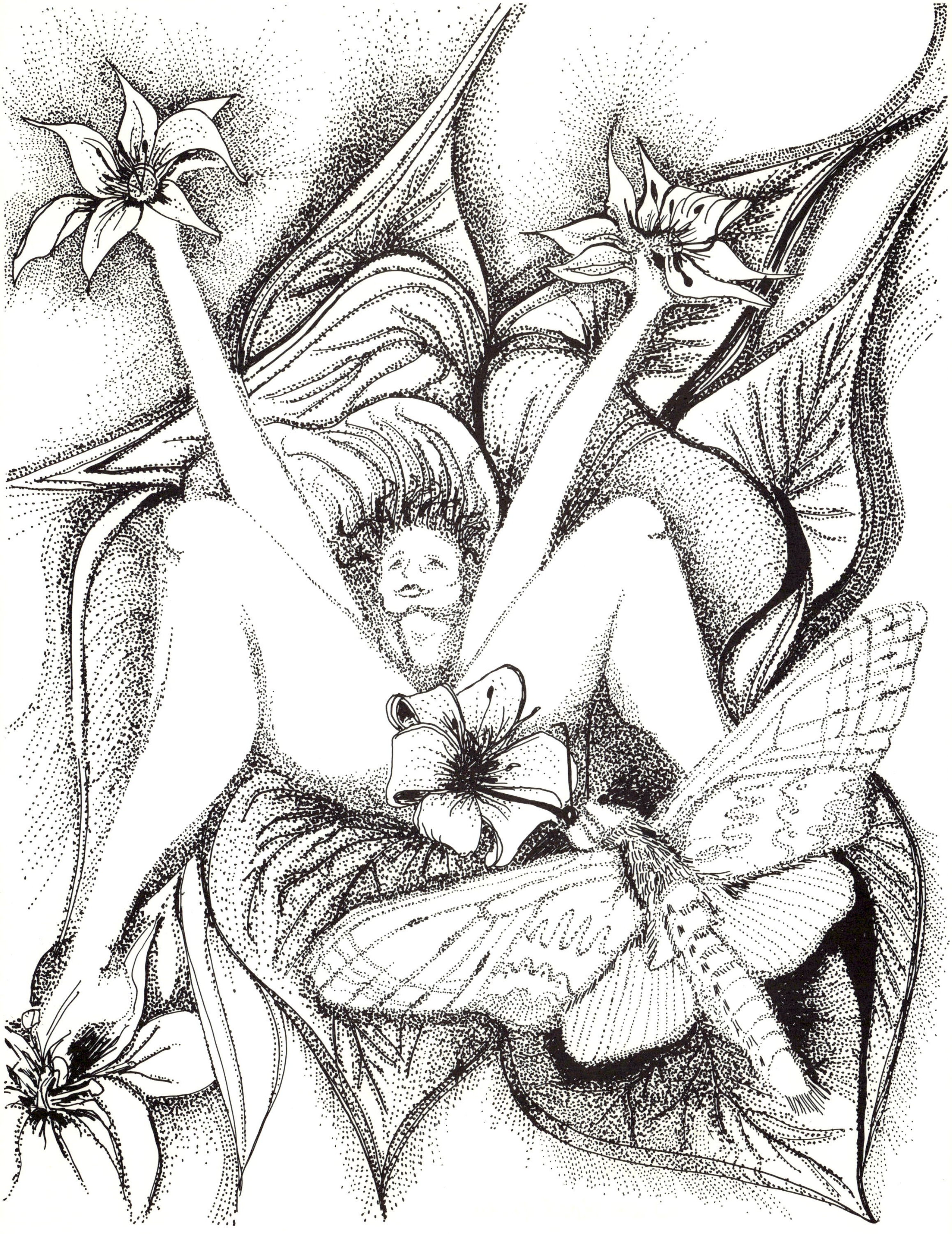

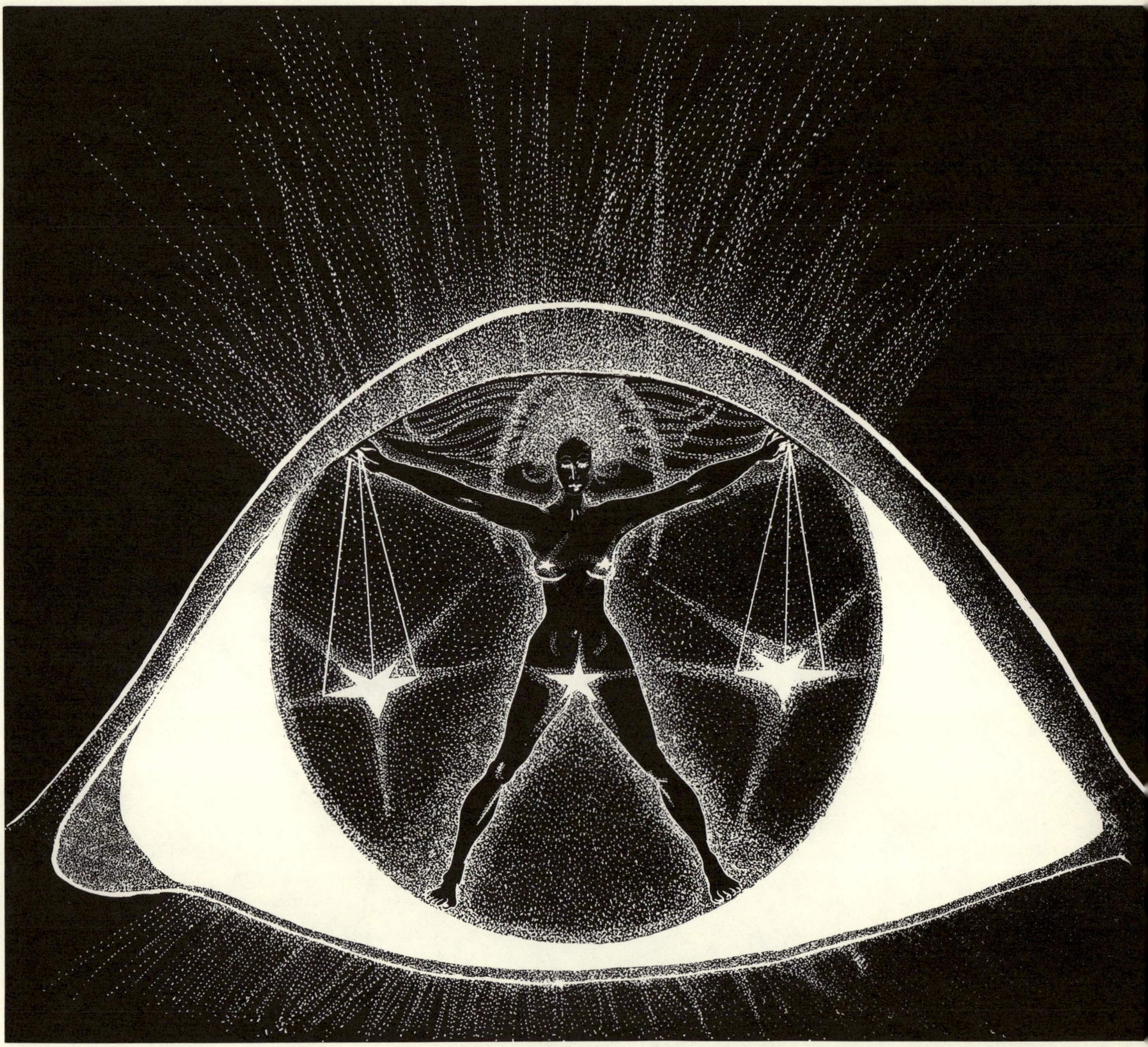

Erotica began as a letter to myself that I believed no one else would ever read. At a moment when I felt most abused by man and his culture, I plunged into my woman's world instead of into defeat. Seeking to discover and affirm what was really mine, I went back to the body.

Moving deeply into the physical, I searched for my spirit. I was attempting to inhabit myself fully, to open into myself and to let the inner woman take flesh. I began to explore my deepest feelings about desire, passion, touching, being touched. When I was lyrical, I accepted it. When I was vulgar, I accepted it. When I was tender, I accepted it. When I was angry, I accepted that too. There was no contradiction between instinct and love when I simply let both flow.

I wrote pages and pages and pages. Often I was exhilarated. Often I was frightened. Often I was doubtful. As I began to let other women writers read what I was doing, their encouragement helped me to keep faith with what I had begun. Fragments, scenes, feelings, memories, images poured forth until I knew the time had to come to shape the spontaneous writing into a work that could be shared with others. That shaping took one year.

Sex energy is life energy is creative energy, and it naturally seeks union. For me the real meaning of *Erotica* came when my words were taken up by artist Adele Aldridge and calligrapher Moira Collins. Each of them responded intensely to my work, then expanded it into other forms of art, and the images continuously changed and grew.

Now *Erotica* is a book made by all three of us; and each word, the letters of each word even, have been touched and loved by a woman's hand.

Donna Ippolito

DONNA IPPOLITO writes feminist history, reviews, criticism and fiction which has appeared in various little magazines. She was a co-founder and editor of *Black Maria,* a feminist quarterly magazine, from 1968 to 1972.

When I was small, I thought pubic hair was called public hair. Although I remember thinking it odd that something so private would be called public, I assumed with only the absurd logic that a catholic schooling can sometimes provide one with, that this inconsistency was somehow related to the same linguistic phenomenon whereby public schools in England were really private.

My confusion about what was private and public about sexual matters was compounded by the fact that my few actual queries about sex were not answered. I can remember asking, while memorizing the ten commandments, what is adultery? I was told that that question was to be answered in the slide presentation that was to follow. Imagine my confusion when the slide for the mortal sin of adultery flashed on the screen, it was a picture of a milk bottle being adulterated by a hand which was pouring water into its mouth.

Given my upbringing, I found it ironic that when I began lettering *Erotica*, I left the manuscript in my living room by accident when I was called to the phone. There it was found by a young nun who was visiting her sister who was staying with us for the month. I didn't realize it had been found until one day when the sister came into my study while I was lettering a page of *Erotica* at my drafting table. When she saw what I was working on, she said something to the effect of, "Oh, so that's why you had that out in the front room, I told my sister that I was sure you wouldn't be *reading* anything like that." Suddenly, visions of milk bottles started dancing in my head, and I was swept back over the years to the ridiculous ratiocinations of my youth, and I thought how odd it was that it would be all right for me to be lettering *Erotica,* but god forbid that I be reading it.

So it is with great pleasure that I announce a la Berryman, "In a state of chortle sin live I," and that not only did I letter *Erotica*, but I read every word of it. And I thank Donna for finally solving my childhood confusions by making the private pubic more public.

Moira Collins

MOIRA COLLINS is a calligrapher with particular interest in commonplace books and the making of individual books, believing with Anais Nin that: "There is only the meaning we give to our individual lives, a book for each person."

My drawings in *Erotica* are a response to the recognition of the courage of Donna Ippolito's poetic and naked writing. They are not intended to arouse, but are an expression of my feelings about man, woman, love and sex. I expect some people will misunderstand *Erotica* because we all have different feelings.

I had to search to find what my feelings were, to let myself express them and not make literal drawings of Donna's words. I felt the fear of rejection, that people would say I was too romantic, not specific enough, and not understand what I meant. I had to let go of that fear if I was going to create anything worthwhile. In the letting go I realized fully how women have been trained to please, to evade, to fake responses. We have been afraid of not being accepted, of not being loved or wanted. It is important to make our own statements, even if they differ from woman to woman. It is time to let ourselves be known as we are, not as other's fantasies of us.

For me, making love and making art are about passion, rapture, roots, growth, regeneration, explosions . . . the cosmos. I often feel sexual energy while drawing and creative energy when making love. In making the drawings for *Erotica* I had to draw from my sexual/sensual/sensory self.

I know that a woman's imagery is not man's. Should it be? I thought about how in the intimacy of sex it is necessary to allow one's self to be vulnerable. I now see that Donna's words, Moira's writing of those words, and my drawings are our individual acts of vulnerability. Publishing **Erotica** is an act of growth towards our own self acceptance.

Adele Aldridge

ADELE ALDRIDGE is the author of *NOTPOEMS* (visual poetry) and *ONCE I WAS A SQUARE, A Visual Fable For Children, Adults & Squares*. A painter, printmaker, poet and graphic designer, she has produced a variety of creative works inspired by the *I CHING*: a series of paintings, black and white graphic symbols, and an artists book hand printed in color in an edition of 55 called, *CHANGES*.

Adele Aldridge's present involvement with the *I CHING* is an intensive interpretation with drawings and words for each line called, *I CHING MEDITATIONS*. This new work reflects her woman's consciousness with her insistence on removing sexism from the *I CHING*. She says, "The *I CHING*, as it now reads, is full of *the superior man* and *the woman in her place*. I am fascinated with the magic and philosophy of these ancient archetypal images and want to restore their meaning to all — from whence they came."

I CHING MEDITATIONS, by Adele Aldridge: a visual and written interpretation of the *I CHING*. The artist has typeset and printed a portfolio for the first three Hexagrams of the *I CHING* in editions of 180, signed and numbered, on Strathmore doubleweight paper. Each portfolio contains 7 prints, 2 or more in color; size 11" X 17", cover 12" X 19". Hexagram number 1, *THE CREATIVE*, Hexagram number 2, *THE RECEPTIVE,* and Hexagram number 3, *DIFFICULTY AT THE BEGINNING* are available from Artists & Alchemists Publications, $30.00 each.